Dirty Bertie

DINOSAUR!

For Merv ~ D R

For Spike and Rudy ~ A M

STRIPES PUBLISHING
An imprint of Little Tiger Press
1 The Coda Centre, 189 Munster Road,
London SW6 6AW

A paperback original
First published in Great Britain in 2013

Characters created by David Roberts
Text copyright © Alan MacDonald, 2013
Illustrations copyright © David Roberts, 2013

ISBN: 978-1-84715-374-6

Dirty Bertie

DINOSAUR!

DAVID ROBERTS WRITTEN BY ALAN MACDONALD

Stripes

Collect all the
Dirty Bertie books!

Contents

CHAPTER 1

"Whiffer, here boy. HERE!" cried Bertie.

Whiffer streaked across the park and vanished into the trees. Bertie rolled his eyes. It was always like this. As soon as Whiffer escaped his lead he zoomed off like a hairy torpedo.

Luckily, Darren and Eugene had come to help.

Dirty Bertie

"Where's he gone?" groaned Darren.

"No idea," said Bertie. "He's probably seen a squirrel or something."

They found Whiffer under the trees, wagging his tail excitedly. He was scrabbling at something in the dirt.

Bertie bent down to pick it up. "Look at this!" he cried.

"What is it? Some sort of bone?" asked Darren.

Bertie rubbed off some of the dirt. "It's a tooth," he said.

"Pretty large one," said Eugene. "Maybe it's a wolf's fang?"

Bertie shook his head. "Too big," he said. "That's a *dinosaur* tooth!"

"No way!" said Darren.

"How do you know?" asked Eugene.

"I've seen pictures," said Bertie. "In my *Dangerous Book of Dinosaurs.*"

"Miss Boot says dinosaurs are extinct," said Eugene. "That tooth could be millions of years old."

Bertie frowned. "It doesn't look millions of years old."

"It must be," said Darren. "Unless a dinosaur was round here recently."

Bertie looked up. He had always dreamed of seeing an actual dinosaur – a Stegosaurus or maybe a Tyrannosaurus rex.

"Maybe they're not all extinct," he said.

"What!" Darren frowned. "You mean there's one living in the park?"

"I'm not saying there is," said Bertie. "But if I was a dinosaur, this is exactly the kind of place I'd hide."

They looked around uneasily. Suddenly the park didn't seem such a safe place.

"Hey, look at this!" cried Eugene. He pointed to some deep scratches on the bark of a tree.

"A dog could have done that," said Darren.

"Yes – or something much bigger," said Bertie.

Eugene shivered. "Um … maybe we should get back," he said.

"Good idea," said Darren. "Before it gets dark."

Dirty Bertie

Bertie put Whiffer on his lead. As they hurried out of the trees they bumped into Angela Nicely. Bertie groaned.

Angela lived next door and was always trailing around after him. Only last week she'd turned up at his house asking if he wanted to play.

"I knew it was you!" she trilled. "What are you doing?"

"Nothing," said Bertie, hiding the dinosaur tooth behind his back.

"I've been watching," said Angela. "You found something."

"Only some old ants' nest," said Bertie quickly.

Angela shook her head. "Liar," she said. "Was it treasure?"

"No," said Bertie.

"I bet it was," said Angela.

"It wasn't," said Bertie. "Oh look, I think your friends want you."

Angela glanced back at the swings where Maisie and Laura were waiting. Bertie took the chance to slip the tooth into his pocket – but Angela saw.

"What's that?" she demanded.

"What?"

"That, in your pocket. Show me!"

Dirty Bertie

"It's nothing," said Bertie. "Anyway we've got to get back."

He hurried after Darren and Eugene.

Angela watched them go. Bertie was definitely hiding something. It was some sort of secret. Well, she would find out — if there was one thing she loved, it was a secret.

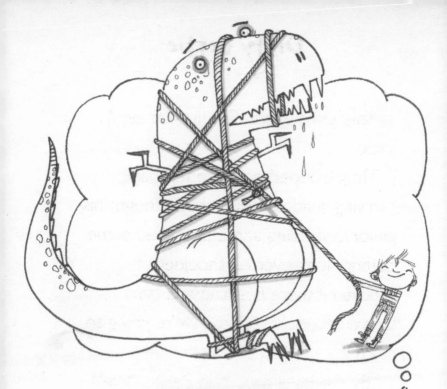

CHAPTER 2

On Saturday morning, Bertie waited
excitedly for Darren and Eugene to
arrive. He was determined to prove
there really was a dinosaur living in the
park. And if there was, he wanted to be
the one to catch it. Imagine capturing
the last dinosaur on earth! They'd be
rich! They'd be famous! He could charge

people ten pounds a go to ride on its back!

They trooped down to the park, carrying spades. Eugene had brought his junior binoculars and Darren had some netting slung over his shoulder.

"Even if there *is* a dinosaur," said Darren, "I don't see how we're going to catch it."

"By making a trap," said Bertie. "We'll dig a hole and cover it over with branches and stuff so no one can see it. When the dinosaur comes along, it'll fall right in."

Eugene looked doubtful. "It'll need to be a big hole," he said. "Dinosaurs are massive."

"We'll make it big," said Bertie. "Really big."

They crossed the park and reached

the trees where they'd found the tooth.

Bertie pointed to a muddy clearing. "We'll dig here," he said.

"What if the park keeper comes?" Eugene asked anxiously.

"He won't," said Bertie. "Anyway, he ought to be grateful. If there is a dinosaur, someone should catch it before anyone gets eaten!"

Eugene looked around nervously. Secretly he hoped the dinosaur didn't exist. Maybe the tooth was really just a stone?

They got on with the digging. It took a long time, but at last they'd dug a big hole deep enough to stand in.

Bertie jumped in to test it. "That'll do," he panted, as Darren heaved him out. "Let's cover it up."

They laid branches across the top and
covered them with leaves and clods of
earth. Bertie stood back to admire their
work. No one would ever know the trap
was there. And anyway, he was pretty
sure that dinosaurs were short sighted.

"What about sticks?" said Darren.
"In case it puts up a fight."

They each found a stick then hid in
some bushes to wait.

Ten minutes passed. Eugene scanned
the trees with his binoculars. Darren
complained his leg had gone to sleep.

Suddenly Bertie sat up. "Listen!" he
hissed. "Something's coming!"

They got ready to jump out. Eugene's
heart thumped. He hoped it was a
Diplodocus because they were
vegetarian.

Dirty Bertie

The bushes rustled. Then something stepped into the clearing.

"BERTIE! WHERE ARE YOU?"

Bertie groaned. Not Angela again!

"What do *you* want?" he cried, coming out from the bushes.

"Found you!" cried Angela triumphantly. "Are we playing pirates?"

"No!" said Bertie. "And don't come any closer or you'll fall in our trap."

Angela noticed the covered hole and crouched down to inspect it.

"Oooh! Did you make it?" she asked.

Dirty Bertie

"Course we made it," said Bertie. "And now you've seen it, you can go."

"I'm not going till you tell me what it's for," said Angela stubbornly.

Bertie and his friends looked at each other. They knew that threatening Angela with spiders or slugs had no effect.

Eugene sighed. "We're hunting a dinosaur, okay?"

Bertie rolled his eyes. Now they'd *never* get rid of her.

"A *dinosaur*?" cried Angela.

"Not so loud!" said Bertie. "We found one of its teeth so it'll probably come back. Then we can catch it."

Angela shook her head. "You won't," she said matter-of-factly. "Not here."

"Yeah? How would you know?" demanded Darren.

Dirty Bertie

"I've seen it," said Angela.

"Seen it?" said Bertie. "You've seen an *actual real* dinosaur?"

"Yes!" said Angela, beaming at them.

"She's making it up!" snorted Darren.

"No, I'm not," said Angela. "I'll show you if you like. It's not far."

CHAPTER 3

They followed Angela out of the park and a little way down Bertie's road. She stopped outside number twelve.

"Here?" said Bertie.

Mr Monk lived at number twelve and he was Bertie's least favourite person. Mr Monk said Bertie's parents should keep him locked up.

Dirty Bertie

Only last week he'd gone on and on about riding bikes on the pavement. And he was always grumbling about dog's muck on the street as if Whiffer was responsible for all of it. He'd written to the local paper to complain. Twice.

They all crouched down behind the hedge.

"There!" said Angela, pointing to the top window. "See it?"

They raised their heads and stared in amazement. There, peering out from behind the curtain, was a real dinosaur! It had green scales, jagged teeth and hungry eyes that watched the street.

"A Tyrannosaurus!" gasped Bertie.

"I told you," said Angela triumphantly.

"But what's it doing there?" asked Eugene.

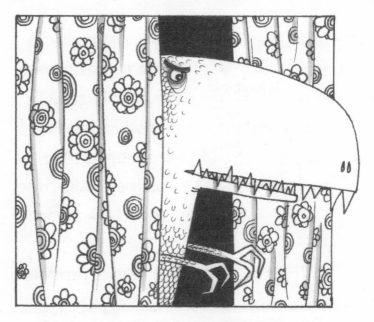

"Maybe it broke in," said Bertie.
"Maybe it got hungry and ate Mr Monk."

"I don't think so," said Darren. "Here he comes."

They ducked down behind the hedge just in time. Mr Monk came marching down the street, carrying a bag. He turned into his drive and unlocked the door to go in.

Dirty Bertie

"Uh oh! Shouldn't we warn him?" whispered Eugene.

"It's a bit late for that," said Bertie.

They waited for Mr Monk to come flying out of the door screaming with terror.

Minutes passed – nothing happened.

Bertie frowned. "You know what I think?" he said. "He's keeping the dinosaur as a pet. I bet he's training it to attack children – especially if they're riding bikes on the pavement."

Angela tugged at his arm. "What shall we do?"

"Capture it," said Bertie. "We've still

got our sticks and the net."

He didn't see why Mr Monk should keep the dinosaur. After all, *he* was the one who'd found the tooth. And besides, it was cruel to keep a dinosaur indoors.

Eugene gulped. "But shouldn't we tell the police?"

Bertie snorted. "The police? You think they'll believe us?"

The others shook their heads. It did sound hard to believe – a Tyrannosaurus living on Fleaman Drive.

"It's up to us," said Bertie. "We've got to get in without old Monk seeing us. Angela, you'll have to keep him busy at the door."

CHAPTER 4

DING DONG!

Angela reached up and rang
Mr Monk's doorbell. She glanced back at
the others and winked with both eyes.
That was the signal.

"Quick! Let's go!" said Bertie.

They slipped through the side gate
and crept round the back of the house.

Dirty Bertie

Mr Monk's back door was open.

Bertie grasped his stick. He couldn't decide which would be scarier – facing a Tyrannosaurus or a hopping mad Mr Monk.

"What if it eats one of us?" whispered Eugene, trembling.

"Don't worry, we'll catch it in the net," said Bertie. "If it grabs you, use your stick."

Darren and Eugene nodded. They followed Bertie in through the back door and tiptoed into the hall.

Mr Monk was outside his front door, hunting for whoever had rung his bell.

Dirty Bertie

They sneaked up the stairs and paused – all was quiet on the landing. Bertie tiptoed over and peeped through the crack of a door.

"It's in there all right," he whispered.

"Couldn't we come back when it's asleep?" pleaded Eugene.

Bertie shook his head. It was now or never. "I'll count to three, then we charge," he said. "One … two … THREE!"

They burst into the room, yelling like savages. The dinosaur was looking out of the window with its back to them. They could see its long tail and scaly green head. Darren ran and threw the net. Then they attacked with their sticks.

YARGH!

CRACK!

CRUMP!

The dinosaur wobbled and toppled over. As it hit the floor, its head broke into pieces.

Darren stepped back. "I think we killed it!" he panted.

Bertie gasped. "It's not dead! It's a model – made of paper and stuff!"

They had really done it this time. Suddenly the door burst open.

"What do you think you're doing?" growled Mr Monk.

Dirty Bertie

"Um … we can explain," mumbled Bertie, backing away.

Mr Monk caught sight of the dinosaur. "My Tyrannosaurus!" he howled. He sunk to his knees with a moan. "It took me *weeks* to make this! It was going on display in Pudsley Museum!"

Bertie picked up a piece of green head. "Maybe you can glue it back together?" he said feebly.

Mr Monk glared. His face had gone purple, his moustache twitched. "YOU … YOU VANDALS!" he snarled. "Wait till I get my hands on you!"

Bertie didn't wait. He fled down the stairs, with Darren and Eugene hot on his heels. Mr Monk chased them on to the street, where Angela was waiting.

"RUN!" yelled Bertie. "RUN!"

The three of them fled down the
road, with Angela trying to catch up.

"Wait! WAIT FOR ME!" she wailed.

Eugene glanced over his shoulder.
"He's still coming!" he gasped.

"Make for the park," panted Bertie.
"We can hide in the trees!"

They dashed in through the gates and
raced past the playground. Bertie
plunged into the trees. He was running

so fast, he forgot to look where he was going. Suddenly the ground gave way beneath him…

CRASH!

He landed in a hail of earth and branches. Seconds later Darren and Eugene fell on top of him.

"OWWW! OOOF!"

They sat up, struggling to untangle their arms and legs.

"What happened?" groaned Eugene.

"We've fallen in our trap!" cried
Darren.

They looked up.

"I think we lost him," panted Eugene.

"Yes, but there's just one problem," said
Bertie. "How are we going to get out?"

They looked at each other. The hole
was deeper than Bertie remembered.

"ANG-ER-LA!" they yelled.

A head appeared, smiling down at
them.

"Oh dear, are you stuck?" asked
Angela.

"Of course we're stuck!" cried Bertie.
"Help us out!"

Angela glanced back over her shoulder.
Mr Monk was coming their way. "Sorry,"
she said. "I'm a bit busy right now…"

CHAPTER 1

Miss Boot stood in front of Class 3.

"As you know, our Spring Fair is this Saturday," she said. "Who's remembered to bring something for the stalls?"

Every hand went up – all except Bertie's because he was picking his nose. Miss Boot went round collecting toys, books, games, knitted booties and

pots of jam. Know-All Nick handed her a
box of white hankies.

"Thank you, Nicholas," said Miss Boot.
"Bertie, what have you brought?"

"Uhh?" said Bertie.

He fished in his pocket and brought
out a toothbrush.

"This is old," said Miss Boot. "It's been
used."

"I know," said Bertie. "That's why I
don't want it."

A voice sang out from the back of the
class. "Miss Boot! You haven't asked me
what *I've* brought!"

Everyone turned round. Bertie rolled
his eyes. Trust Royston Rich to butt in.
Royston was the world's biggest
show-off. He'd probably brought in a
signed photo of himself.

Dirty Bertie

Royston placed a large box on his desk. Everyone gasped. It was the biggest Easter egg they'd ever seen.

Bertie stared at it, boggle-eyed. It was a whopper, bigger than a football … bigger even than Royston's big head.

"Splendid!" said Miss Boot, picking it up. "I think it's almost too good for the sweet stall."

"It ought to be a prize, Miss," said Donna.

"Ooh yes, we could have a competition!" cried Know-All Nick. "You have to guess the weight and whoever's closest wins the egg!"

Miss Boot nodded. "Do you know, Nicholas, I think that's a *brilliant* idea!"

Dirty Bertie

Nick glowed with pride. Obviously it was a brilliant idea because he had thought of it. Better still, it meant he could get his hands on all that yummy chocolate. He was bound to win the competition because he always came first at everything.

At the back of the class, Bertie hadn't been able to take his eyes off the egg. *Imagine it,* he thought, *a chocolate egg so big you'd need a forklift truck to get it home.* Whatever it took, he had to win — and no one was going to stop him. Not even Know-All Nick.

By break time, word had spread round the whole school. Everyone was talking about the monster egg.

"I'd eat a little bit every day," said Eugene. "It would last for months."

"It'd probably go mouldy," said Darren. "I'd eat it all in one day."

"I'd guzzle it in five minutes," said Bertie. "And then I'd be sick."

"What makes you think you'd get the chance?" sneered a voice.

Bertie swung round. It was that slimy sneak, Know-All Nick. He was always snooping on other people's conversations.

Dirty Bertie

"Who asked you, big nose?" said Bertie.

Nick ignored him. "Face it," he said. "You're never going to win."

"Oh, yeah? Why not?" said Bertie.

"Because obviously *I'm* going to win," boasted Nick.

"Says who?"

"Says me!"

"We'll see about that," said Bertie. "I'm pretty good at guessing."

"Really?" said Nick. "But I won't need to guess because I'm a genius. I can work it out."

Dirty Bertie

"How?" said Bertie.

Nick tapped his nose. "Ahh, wouldn't you like to know?" he smirked. "See you later, losers!"

Bertie watched him go. *Right*, he thought, *this means war. Only one of us can win that egg.* He couldn't wait to see the look on Nick's face when Miss Boot handed him the prize.

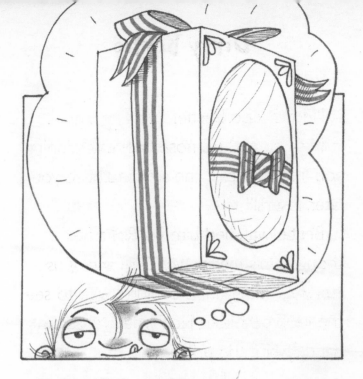

CHAPTER 2

All that morning Bertie couldn't stop
thinking about the giant egg. Miss Boot
had removed it from class because she
was tired of people wanting to hold it.
Everyone was desperate to guess how
much it weighed.

Bertie sighed – he hadn't a clue. But
what if Nick was telling the truth and you

could work it out? Unfortunately, he was rubbish at maths. Subtraction was so tiring and fractions gave him a headache. No, if he was going to win he needed help. But who could he ask? Darren was no use. He got stuck on his three times table. And maths got Eugene muddled.

Hold on, thought Bertie, *if anyone knows the answer, it's Miss Boot.* She was a teacher after all! But how to trick her into giving him a clue? Bertie slipped out of his seat and made his way to the front.

"Miss," he said. "Can I ask a question?"

"No. Sit down," snapped Miss Boot. "Get on with your work."

"This *is* about work," said Bertie. "I was thinking about maths."

Miss Boot gawped. Was Bertie ill? Usually he avoided maths like the plague.

"Well, what is it?" she said.

"I was just wondering," said Bertie. "Are big things heavier than smaller things?"

Miss Boot sighed. "I've no idea what you're talking about."

"Well, like for instance, how much do *you* weigh?" asked Bertie.

"ME?" said Miss Boot.

"I don't mean exactly," said Bertie quickly. "I mean, roughly, do you weigh a ton or more?"

"A TON!" screeched Miss Boot, sounding as if she might explode. Bertie gulped. This wasn't going as well as he'd hoped.

"What about smaller things?" he babbled. "Like toffee or crisps or … chocolate eggs?"

Miss Boot's eyes narrowed. "Has this got something to do with a certain competition?"

"Erm, not really."

"Because let me warn you, Bertie, there will be *no cheating,*" said Miss Boot. "If you think you can weigh that egg, forget it. It's somewhere you'll never find it. Now *sit down.*"

Bertie trailed back to his seat. Some people were so suspicious. He hadn't got any information out of Miss Boot and now she suspected him of cheating.

He'd never even *thought* of weighing the egg. But actually that was a brilliant idea. If he could "borrow" it, he could find out the exact weight. There was just one problem. Where had Miss Boot hidden it? In her handbag? No, not big enough. The book cupboard? Too obvious.

A smile spread across Bertie's face. Of course! It was somewhere he'd never find it … somewhere children were not allowed… THE STAFFROOM!

CHAPTER 3

DRRRRINNG!

The bell rang for lunch break. Bertie shot out of class and flew down the corridor. He only had a minute to carry out his mission before the teachers arrived. He screeched to a halt at the staffroom and peeped round the door. No one was about.

Now … where would Miss Boot hide a giant chocolate egg? He got down on all fours and looked under the coffee table. No luck. Nothing behind the curtains. His eye fell on the cupboard. He threw open the door. EUREKA! THERE IT WAS!

Bertie grabbed the monster egg. Now to weigh it… Argh! Bertie groaned. In his excitement he'd forgotten he'd need some scales.

Suddenly he heard voices in the corridor. Help! If Miss Boot caught him in the staffroom she'd go berserk.

Bertie looked around for somewhere to hide. But where? There was only the coffee table. It was a tight fit, but maybe he could squeeze underneath. He made it just as the door opened.

The room filled up with teachers.
Bertie lay squashed under the table, not
daring to breathe. This was like a horror
film – trapped in a room with killer
zombies! He could see Mr Weakly's shiny
shoes and Miss Boot's baggy stockings
only inches away.

"You know what Bertie asked me
today?" Miss Boot was speaking.

"What?" asked Miss Darling.

"He asked me if I weighed a ton!"

Miss Darling giggled. "That boy! Tee hee!"

"He'll be the death of me," snorted Miss Boot. "Sometimes I think he lives on another planet."

"Sometimes I wish he did," said Mr Weakly.

Bertie almost banged his head. Was this what teachers talked about when they were alone? Him! Didn't they have homework to discuss?

MUNCH, MUNCH…

Bertie groaned. Now they were eating their sandwiches! He could smell cheese and pickle. This was torture. If only he'd brought something to eat!

Then he remembered – he had the chocolate egg. But there was no way he could touch that. It was a prize for the school fair. Miss Boot would blow a fuse. On the other hand, it *was* chocolate … and it was enormous… Who was going to miss a teeny-weeny piece?

Slowly, Bertie slid out the egg from its box. He peeled off the gold paper and broke off a piece. SNAP!

Dirty Bertie

He held his breath. Luckily the teachers
were too busy yakking to hear. Bertie
crammed the chocolate into his mouth.

Mmm, mmm! It was the sweetest,
smoothest chocolate he'd
ever tasted. One
more piece and
then he'd put it away.

"Has anyone seen my glasses case?"
It was Mr Weakly again.

Bertie looked about. By his feet was a
blue glasses case.

"Maybe it's fallen on the floor?" suggested Miss Darling.

Bertie turned cold. If Mr Weakly bent down to look, he'd see him under the table. He had to do something and fast! He gave the glasses case a kick. It shot out from under the table. A moment later a hand reached down.

"It's all right. Found it!" cried Mr Weakly.

Bertie breathed out. That was close. He nibbled more chocolate to calm his nerves.

The lunch hour dragged on. Bertie's neck ached from lying squashed under the table. His hands were sweating. Only chocolate kept him going. At long last the bell rang.

Bertie waited until he was certain the last teacher had gone and crawled out.

There wasn't time to weigh the egg
now. He had to put it back and return
to class. He looked down and gasped.

YIKES! Who'd scoffed half the egg?
He must have gobbled it without even
knowing. What was he going to do?

Dirty Bertie

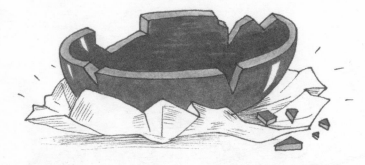

Miss Boot would go bonkers if she found out. Bertie wrapped up the half-eaten egg and slid it back in the box. Wait a minute… Only the front half of the egg was showing, which still looked smooth and perfect. No one would guess! He was saved!

He stuffed the Easter egg back in the cupboard. Now to whizz back to class before Miss Boot missed him. He licked his lips. Hmm, first he'd better wipe the chocolate off his face.

CHAPTER 4

The day of the Spring Fair was bright and sunny. The school playground was crowded with people. Many of Bertie's class were in charge of stalls.

By far the most popular was the Giant Easter Egg competition run by Miss Boot. The egg stood proudly on the table in its gold box. People queued to pay fifty pence to guess the weight. Miss Boot's cash box was stuffed with coins and notes. In five minutes she had promised to announce the winner.

Bertie and his friends sucked lollipops as they watched.

"I never win anything," sighed Eugene.

"Someone has to win," said Darren.

Bertie shrugged. "It's only an Easter egg," he said.

"Are you kidding?" said Darren. "It's massive! It's the biggest chocolate egg in history!"

"Yes," said Eugene. "Imagine taking the first bite."

Well, maybe not the first, thought Bertie, *because I already scoffed half of it.* He hoped Miss Boot would hurry up. Maybe he'd be the winner? He'd made a guess like everyone else – there was no sense in not entering. Someone poked him in the back. Bertie turned round to see his enemy, Know-All Nick.

"I hope you're not going to cry, Bertie," he jeered.

"Cry?" said Bertie. "What for?"

"When I win the competition," said Nick.

"What makes you so sure?" asked Bertie.

"I told you," said Nick. "I'm a genius. I worked it out."

Miss Boot was heading to the microphone. Bertie joined the crowd to hear the result. Whoever won was in for a bit of a surprise. But he wasn't worried. No one could pin the blame on him.

"And now, the result of our Giant Easter Egg competition," said Miss Boot. "There were a huge number of entries but the winner is…" She looked up. "Nicholas!"

Dirty Bertie

Bertie laughed. Who else? Know-All Nick wouldn't be smiling so much when he unwrapped his prize.

Nick made his way to the front as people clapped.

Miss Boot handed over the golden egg. "Well done, Nicholas," she said. "Your guess was exactly right."

"Huh, how amazing," said Bertie.

"Yeah," grumbled Darren. "I bet he cheated."

Nick made straight towards them, eager to enjoy his triumph. "I told you," he gloated. "I'm a genius!"

"You cheated," said Bertie.

"Not really," said Nick. "I used my brain. It turns out Spillers are selling this Easter egg in their shop. So I popped in and asked what it weighed."

"Like I said, you cheated," said Bertie.

Nick licked his lips. "Never mind, Bertie. As a special treat, you can watch me eat it."

"Now?" said Bertie.

"Why not?" said Nick. "I've got masses of chocolate, so I can eat it any time I like."

Dirty Bertie

He slid the giant egg out of the box and greedily tore off the wrapper. His face turned a ghastly white.

"NOOOOOOOO!" he wailed. "SOMEONE'S EATEN IT!"

"No! Really?" said Bertie, trying not to smile.

Nick spun round to face him. Only one person could have done this. "YOU ATE IT!" he cried. "I'm telling!"

Bertie gave a shrug.

"But Nickerless, how could I?" he said. "Miss Boot had it locked away. No one could have touched that egg. Well, not unless they were a genius!"

CHAPTER 1

Bertie was in the kitchen doing his homework. He sighed loudly. How was he meant to concentrate when Mum and Mrs Nicely kept talking?

He hoped she hadn't come round to invite him to one of Angela's parties. Last time it had turned out to be just him and a dozen girls in fairy costumes.

Dirty Bertie

"…So, we're going to my sister's for the weekend," Mrs Nicely was saying. "But I can't think what to do about Pusskins. Normally Mrs Crab feeds him, but she's in hospital."

"Oh dear," said Mum.

"Exactly," said Mrs Nicely. "I'm really in a fix. In fact, I was wondering if you might do it?"

"I'd be glad to," said Mum, "but I've got a lot on this weekend. What about Bertie?"

"ME?" Bertie looked up from doodling a picture of Miss Boot.

Dirty Bertie

Mrs Nicely frowned. She was hoping to find someone sensible. Bertie was about as sensible as a jelly sandwich.

"Well, I don't know," she said doubtfully. "Are you good with cats?"

"Not especially," said Bertie. "I'm good with dogs."

Bertie didn't mind cats, but he didn't really see the point of them. All they did was sleep, laze around and eat. You couldn't take a cat for a walk or throw a ball for it to fetch. Pusskins was too fat and idle to fetch anything. Anyway, he didn't see why *he* had to feed him.

Mrs Nicely sighed. "Well, it would be doing me a great favour. And, of course, I'd pay you."

"PAY ME?" cried Bertie. "How much?"

"BERTIE!" groaned Mum.

"It's all right," said Mrs Nicely. "Let's see, what about five pounds?"

FIVE POUNDS? Bertie almost fell off his chair. That was more than double his pocket money! And all for feeding a fat moggy. Yippee! He was going to be rich!

Bertie followed Mrs Nicely next door so she could explain what he had to do. Angela was in the kitchen practising her ballet. She ran upstairs and came back with Pusskins, who lolled in her arms like a furry pudding.

"Here he is!" she trilled. "This is Bertie. Say hello, Pusskins."

Bertie reached out a hand.

"Grrrrr!" snarled the cat, arching his back.

"He likes having his tummy tickled," said Angela. "You have to feed him twice a day and he only likes Kitty Krunch."

Fusspot, thought Bertie. Whiffer would eat anything – even the pizza off your plate.

"When does he go out?" he asked.

"After tea and only in the back garden," said Angela. "Mostly he sleeps on my bed, don't you, Pussypops?"

Mrs Nicely showed Bertie the cat food and gave him a front door key.

"One more thing," she said. "Don't forget to turn off the burglar alarm."

"Burglar alarm?" said Bertie. No one had mentioned this before! Mrs Nicely showed him a panel by the door with rows of buttons.

"It's quite simple," she said. "You just punch in the code to turn it on or off – four-two-seven. Can you remember that?" Bertie nodded. "Repeat it to me."

"Four … seven … umm…"

Mrs Nicely rolled her eyes. "I'll write it down for you," she said. "And lock the door when you leave. Have you got all that?"

"Yes," said Bertie. "Do the alarm, feed the cat and lock the door."

"Don't forget," warned Mrs Nicely. "The alarm's linked to the police station so it must be turned off immediately."

She watched Bertie stuff the key in his pocket. Possibly she was out of her mind – this was, after all, the boy who'd arrived at Angela's party dressed as a worm. But it was too late to find someone else. All he had to do was feed a cat – surely even Bertie could manage that?

CHAPTER 2

BEEP! BEEP! BEEP!

It was Saturday morning. Bertie had let himself in to the Nicelys' house and the burglar alarm was going mad. *ARGH! Quick! Where's that piece of paper?* He found it in his pocket and hurriedly punched in the code.

BEEP! BEEP! BE—The alarm stopped.

Dirty Bertie

Bertie let out a sigh of relief. Why did the Nicelys need a burglar alarm anyway? Why didn't they just get a guard dog?

He went into the kitchen and filled the cat bowl with Kitty Krunch.

"PUSSKINS!" he called. "Look what I've got!"

The fat grey cat appeared in the doorway and plodded into the kitchen. It glared at Bertie then sniffed the food as if it might be rat poison. Bertie glanced around the kitchen – suddenly it dawned on him that he had the Nicelys' house all to himself. He could do whatever he liked! He could watch TV with his feet up or help himself to biscuits. He could bounce on all the beds. Come to think

of it, he'd never seen Angela's bedroom.
Maybe he'd have a quick nose around.

Bertie crept upstairs. Angela's bedroom
had pink walls with pink curtains and a
pink duvet covered in hearts.

YUCK! thought Bertie. He flopped on
to the bed. Wouldn't Angela be furious if
she could see him now? It would serve
her right for telling everyone he was her
boyfriend. He looked at Angela's books.
They had titles like *My Cuddly Kitten Gets
Lost* and *Girls 4 Ever!* He took down a
sparkly exercise book. On the cover
were the words: MY STORIES by Angela
Nicely – Strickly Private.

Ah ha! thought Bertie. What was so
private that Angela didn't want anyone
reading it? He opened the book at the
first story.

Once upon a time there was a beautiful princess called Princess Angela. She lived in a big palace with loads of servants to make her bed and turn on the TV and stuff.

One sunny day Princess Angela was playing in her garden when a prince came by. His name was Prince Bertie and secretly he had fallen in love with Princess Angela…

Dirty Bertie

WHAT?! Bertie threw the book down in disgust. He wanted to be sick. How dare Angela put him in her soppy fairy tale? How dare she make him a drippy prince who went round falling in love and living happily ever after?

What if any of his friends saw the story? Bertie felt ill. What if Angela ever read it out in class? The news would be all round school in no time. People would start calling him Prince Bertie! YUCK!

No, he had to make sure that didn't happen. But how? He could throw the book in the dustbin. But wait, he had a better idea. Why not simply change the story? He could cross out his own name and replace it with someone else – Prince Nickerless for example.

Bertie smiled to himself. Wouldn't Angela be mad when she saw it? He glanced at the clock. Mum would be wondering where he was. Never mind, he'd carry out his brilliant plan later when he gave Pusskins his tea.

CHAPTER 3

BEEP! BEEP! BEEP!

The burglar alarm rang out. It was six o'clock and Bertie was back. As he hurried inside, something shot through his legs like a furry rocket. ARGH! Pusskins had got out! Bertie was just in time to see him vanish over the wall. This was terrible!

Dirty Bertie

Pusskins wasn't meant to go out the front. What if he went missing – or got run over? Mrs Nicely would blame him. Angela would burst into tears, and he could forget about his five pounds.

BEEP! BEEP! The alarm could wait – he had to find that pesky cat. He looked over next-door's wall. "Pusskins! Puss puss!"

No sign of him. Bertie searched up and down the road.

"Pusskins!"

Nothing. He dashed back to the house.

Pusskins was sitting on the doormat, yawning.

Dirty Bertie

Bertie gave him a look.

BEEP! BEEP!

What was that noise? It sounded like
… HELP! – THE BURGLAR ALARM!
What was the number? *Two … four …
umm…?* Bertie fumbled in his pocket for
the piece of paper and punched in the
code. The alarm stopped.

He stood panting for breath. It was a
close thing but everything seemed okay.
Pusskins slunk past him into the kitchen.

Dirty Bertie

Bertie poured out the Kitty Krunch, then hurried upstairs. Angela's storybook was still on the bed. Now to make a few small changes…

Once upon a time there was
a ~~beautiful~~ SMELLY princess called
Princess ~~Angela~~ POOPALOT. She lived in
a big ~~palace~~ DUSTBIN with loads of
~~servants~~ RATS AND MAGGOTS to make her bed and
turn on the TV and stuff.

One sunny day Princess ~~Angela~~ POOPALOT
was playing in her garden when a
prince came by. His name was
Prince ~~Bertie~~ NICKERLESS THE UGLY and secretly he
had fallen in ~~love with Princess~~ A COWPAT
~~Angela~~…

Dirty Bertie

Bertie broke off. What was that noise? It sounded like it came from downstairs. It was probably only Pusskins. He went back to his story.

SLAM!

Bertie froze. Not even Pusskins could slam a door. Help! There was someone in the house. Bertie gulped. What was the use of a burglar alarm if a burglar could just walk in?

CHAPTER 4

Bertie looked around in panic. If he tried to sneak downstairs the burglar might hear him. If only he had his trusty pirate cutlass. But all Angela had in her room was teddies and cuddly rabbits. He grabbed *The Bedtime Book of Fairy Tales*, which was the biggest book on the shelf. Voices were coming from downstairs.

Dirty Bertie

"Find anything?"

"No, nothing."

Bertie broke into a cold sweat. There wasn't one burglar, but two! Maybe if he kept very quiet the crooks wouldn't come upstairs.

CLUMP, CLUMP, CLUMP…

Uh oh. Bertie looked round for somewhere to hide. He slipped behind Angela's bedroom door and held his breath. Footsteps came along the landing.

"You take that one, I'll check in here."

CREAK!

The bedroom door swung back, squashing him against the wall. A big man came into the room. Bertie crept out and raised the book above his head…

THWACK!

"OWW!"

The man fell flat on his face. Bertie stared at his uniform.

"You're the police!" he gasped.

"Of course I'm the police," said the constable. "Oww! That really hurt!"

A sergeant came rushing in.

"He hit me!" grumbled the constable.

"Don't be so soft," said the sergeant. He gripped Bertie's arm. "Right, young man, you'd better come along with us," he said sternly.

"What for?" said Bertie.

"For breaking into this house."

"But I didn't!"

"You set off the burglar alarm. Didn't you hear it?" asked the sergeant.

Bertie stared. Mrs Nicely's words came back to him: the burglar alarm was linked to the police station. He should have turned it off straight away. Now the police thought he was a burglar!

"But I only came to feed the cat!" he protested.

The sergeant laughed. "That's a good one. So why were you hiding?"

"Because I thought *you* were burglars!" wailed Bertie.

"Very funny," said the sergeant. "We'll talk about this at the station."

At the station! *This is a nightmare,*

Dirty Bertie

thought Bertie. *I'll be sent to prison! I'll never see Whiffer again!*

The policemen took him downstairs and outside to the police car.

"That's my house, next door!" cried Bertie.

"Of course it is!" laughed the sergeant, shaking his head.

"No, really, it is!" yelled Bertie. "You can ask my mum!"

The policemen looked at each other. The boy did seem a bit young for a burglar. Maybe it was best to be on the safe side. They rang the doorbell.

Dirty Bertie

Mum came to the door. Her eyes almost popped out of her head when she saw Bertie with two policemen.

"Sorry to bother you, madam. Do you know this boy?" asked the sergeant.

"I should do," said Mum. "He's my son. What's he done now?"

Bertie threw back his head. "NOTHING!" he howled. "THAT'S WHAT I KEEP TELLING THEM!"

Dirty Bertie

It took about half an hour and two cups of tea to explain the whole story. Luckily, the sergeant saw the funny side. He said that in future Bertie should be kept away from burglar alarms. And he better not make a habit of belting policemen over the head.

When they'd gone, Mum rounded on him. "I thought you knew how to work the alarm!" she fumed.

"I did!" said Bertie. "It was Pusskins's fault. He ran off!"

Mum folded her arms. "Well, I don't know what Mrs Nicely will say," she said.

"She doesn't have to know, does she?" said Bertie.

"No," said Mum grimly. "Maybe we'll keep it that way."

Dirty Bertie

On Sunday the Nicelys returned.
Mrs Nicely came round with Angela.

"Thank you so much for feeding
Pusskins," she said. "I hope everything
was all right?"

"Um, yes, fine," mumbled Bertie.

"Good. And no problems with the
burglar alarm?"

Bertie looked at Mum.

"No, no problems at all," she said.

"Marvellous!" said Mrs Nicely. "Well,
thank you, Bertie, you've been a great
help."

She stuffed something into his hand
and went on chatting. Bertie looked.
A five-pound note! He could buy
hundreds of—

EH? The money was grabbed from his
hand.

"I'll take that, thank you," said Angela.

"W-what?" said Bertie. "But it's mine!"

Angela shook her head. "I need a new storybook," she said. "Someone scribbled in mine."

"Oh, did they?" said Bertie.

Angela narrowed her eyes. "Don't be stupid. I know it was you."

Bertie sighed. He should have seen this coming. "Okay, I'll make a deal," he said. "Half each."

Angela shook her head. "No thanks!
I'll keep it all. Unless you want me to tell
my mum."

Bertie's shoulders drooped. He knew
when he was beaten. In future he was
having nothing to do with cats.

"Oh, by the way," said Angela, on her
way out. "I'm starting on a new story.
It's called Bertie Ballerina!"